Text and illustrations copyright © 2015 by Rebecca Emberley Inc.
A Neal Porter Book
Published by Roaring Brook Press
Roaring Brook Press is a division of Holtzbrinck Publishing Holdings Limited Partnership
175 Fifth Avenue, New York, New York 10010
The artwork for this book was created using cut paper and digital techniques.
mackids.com

Library of Congress Cataloging-in-Publication Data

Emberley, Rebecca.
  Spare parts / Rebecca Emberley, Ed Emberley. — First edition.
    pages cm
  "A Neal Porter book."
  Summary: While searching for a replacement heart at the Spare Parts Mart,
a lonely robot finds a friend.
  ISBN 978-1-59643-723-4 (hardback)
[1. Stories in rhyme. 2. Robots—Fiction. 3. Loneliness—Fiction. 4.
Friendship—Fiction.] I. Emberley, Ed. II. Title.
  PZ8.3.E517Sp 2015
  [E]—dc23
                                              2014044215

Roaring Brook Press books may be purchased for business or promotional use. For information
on bulk purchases please contact Macmillan Corporate and Premium Sales Department
at (800) 221-7945 x5442 or by email at specialmarkets@macmillan.com.

First edition 2015
Book design by Andrew Arnold
Printed in China by Toppan Leefung Printing Ltd., Dongguan City, Guangdong Province

10 9 8 7 6 5 4 3 2 1

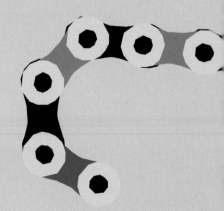

Rebecca Emberley and Ed Emberley

PARTS

A NEAL PORTER BOOK
ROARING BROOK PRESS
New York

Meet Rhoobart.

Tarnished and tattered,
He felt nothing mattered.
He was all spare parts,
With a secondhand heart.

All of his days were lonely and boring.

Until today.

Today, as Rhoobart shook off the rusty dust of sleep
And checked all his gears and whizzers,
He found that his heart would not start.

He gave it a crank, he gave it a yank . . .
He tried twisting and turning
But nothing—not a tick not a tock.
His heart just would not start.

Rhoobart jumped,
Then he bumped,
Then he thumpity thumped,
And still,
His heart would not start.

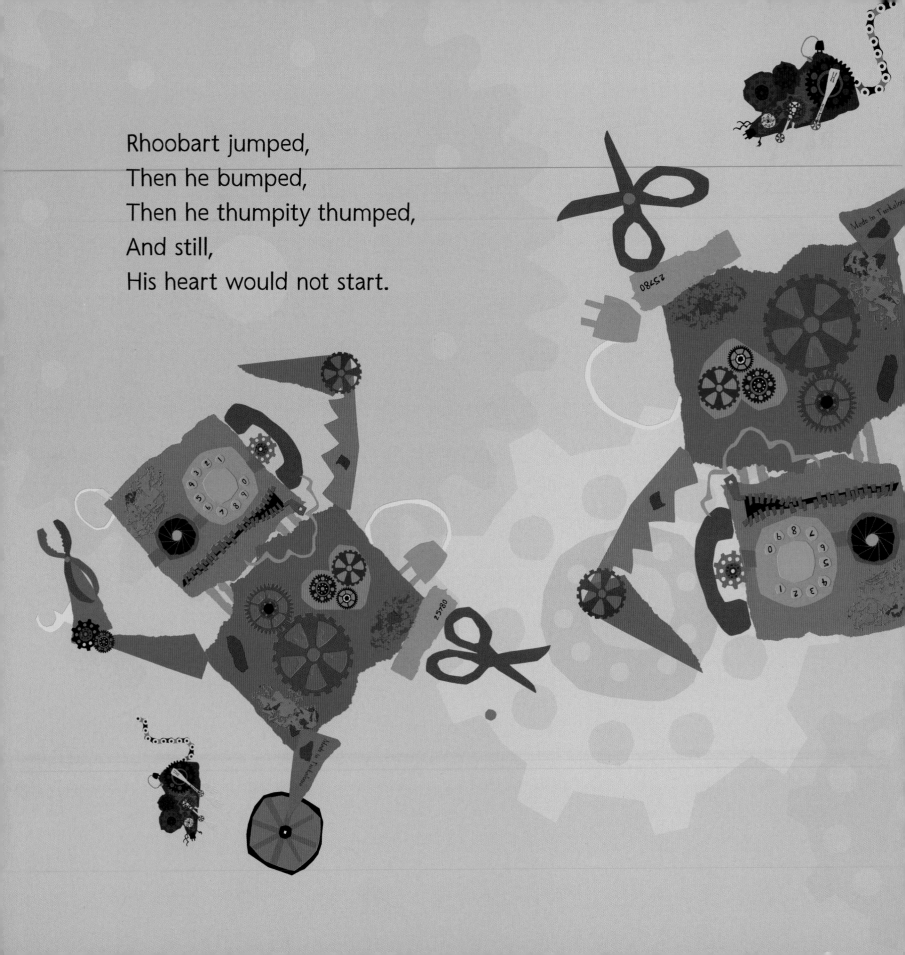

He would have to go
To the Spare Parts Mart
To sort out a new heart.
The thought made him feel wobbly.

Meet Blaggart.

Owner of the Spare Parts Mart.
He lives in a box,
And smells of old socks.

"Whadya want?" Blaggart rasped.

Rhoobart's rusty old parts rattled and clanked.
He tried not to notice how much Blaggart stank.
He adjusted his gears and held back his tears.

"Heart," he croaked.

In case of emergency

Open Here

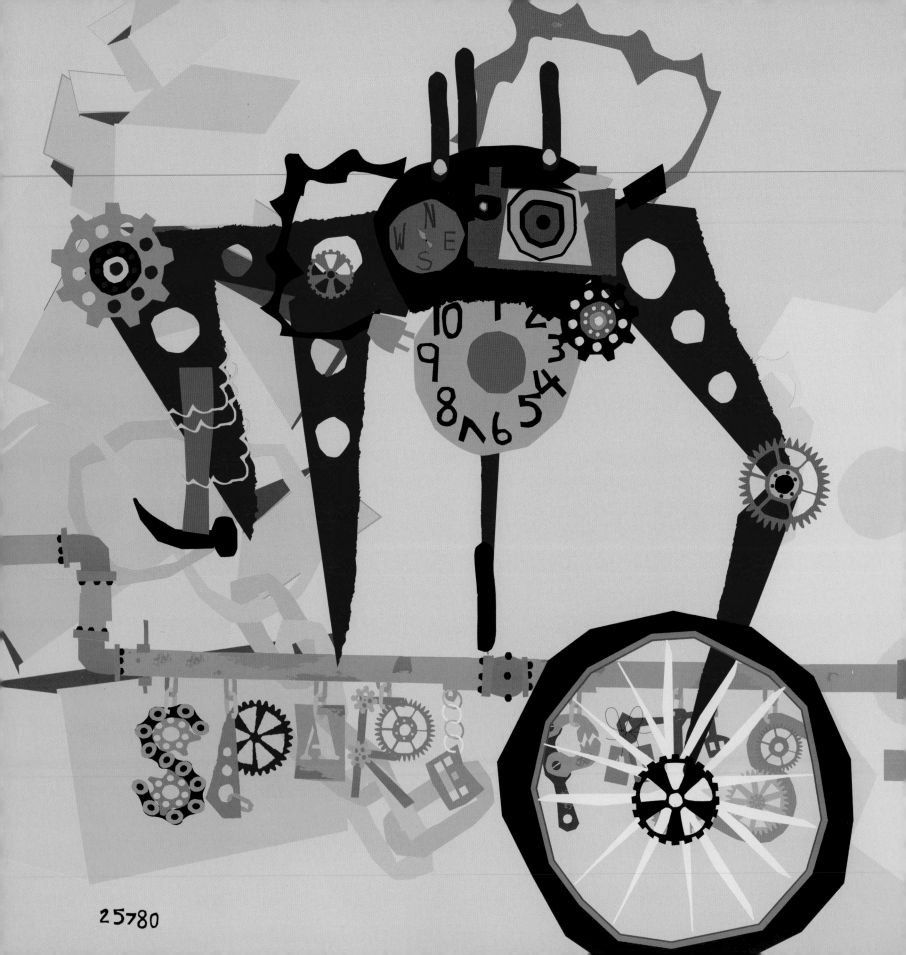

"Part?" shouted Blaggart, "WHAT PART?
WE GOT LOTS O' PARTS!"

"HEART!" Rhoobart groaned.

"Arrrgh, I don't know what you're after
   you silly bit of rust," Blaggart growled.
You'll have to go out back
And forage for yourself.
Just watch out for Mozart."

"Mozart?" asked Rhoobart.

"MOZART!" Blaggart screeched,
as he wheeled himself away.

Rhoobart dug into the rubble
And he rummaged through the junk.
He came upon a jukebox,
Which he gave a little thunk.

"Can you help me?" he creaked.

It made a click, then a whir.
What that meant he wasn't sure,
So he moved on.

MAIL

pick up 10:00

pick up 3:30

3 different = you lose
3 the same = you still lose

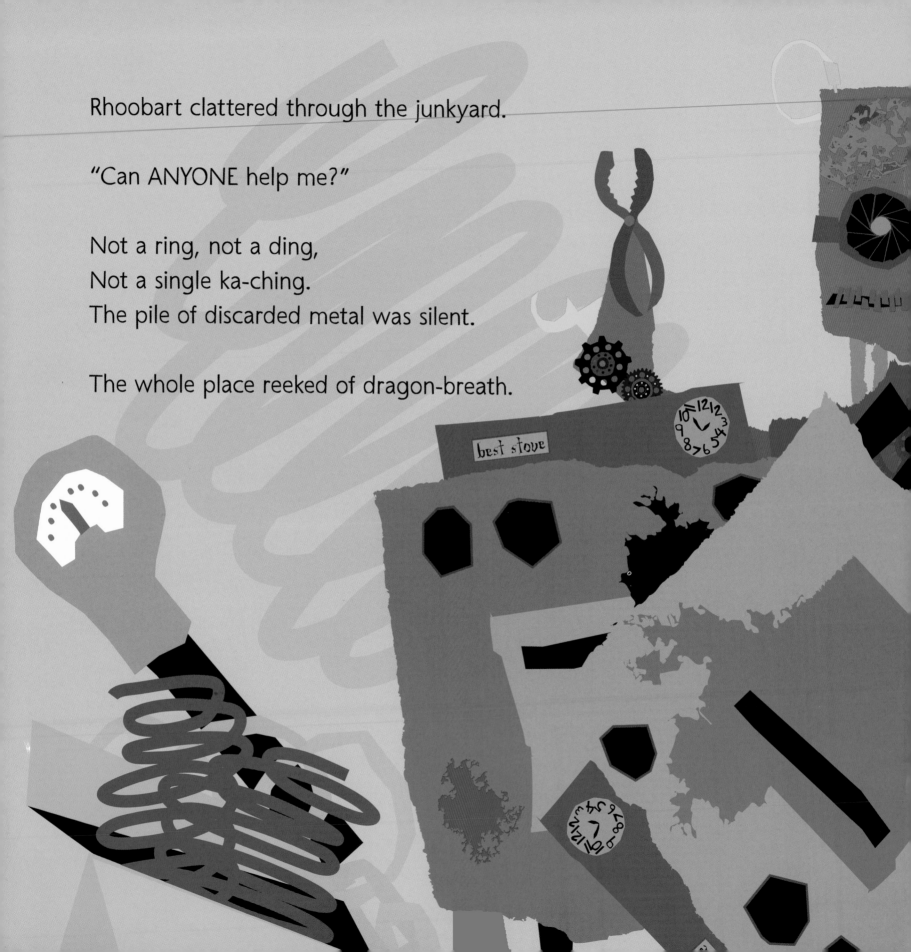

Rhoobart clattered through the junkyard.

"Can ANYONE help me?"

Not a ring, not a ding,
Not a single ka-ching.
The pile of discarded metal was silent.

The whole place reeked of dragon-breath.

best stove

Meet Mozart.

YEEEEEK!

He scared Rhoobart to pieces
But STILL—
His heart did not start.

Rhoobart gave up.
He lay down in the dark.
His zippery lips chattered,
He rattled and clattered.
Now he was sure NOTHING mattered.

25780

Made in Tuskaloos.

Meet Sweetart.

An energetic bit of metal
With just the right amount of tarnish.

"Why are you lying here in the dark?"

"Heart won't start," croaked Rhoobart.
"Need new heart."

"Nonsense," she crooned.
"You don't need a new heart,
    you just need a jump start!"

With one quick spark
She jump-started his heart.
With a clank and a clunk,
It started to thump.

"Ah," Rhoobart thought,
"THIS is what matters!"

We're all spare parts.
We've got secondhand hearts,
It's true.

We go together like pickles and glue.

You stick to me,
I'll stick to you.

We're tarnished and tattered,
But it doesn't matter.
You stick to me and I'll stick to you.